P9-CMT-341

DRIVING LESSONS

Also By Ed McBain

DRIVING LESSONS

Ed McBain

An Otto Penzler Book

CARROLL & GRAF PUBLISHERS, INC.

NEW YORK

First Carroll & Graf edition 2000
Second Printing November 2000

Carroll & Graf Publishers, Inc.
A Division of Avalon Publishing Group
19 West 21st Street
New York, NY 10010-6805

Library of Congress Cataloging-in-Publication Data is available.

ISBN: 0-7867-0805-0

Manufactured in the United States of America

DRIVING LESSONS

The girl looked sixteen and blonde, and the man looked thirty-two and dazed. The responding blues were questioning the girl and trying to question the man who'd been in the vehicle. They weren't expecting much from the man, not in his condition.

They thought at first he was drunk even though he didn't smell of alcohol. The girl was cold sober. Hysterical because she'd just run somebody over, but cold sober nonetheless. She was the one who'd been driving the car.

'What's your name, miss?' one of the blues asked.

'Rebecca Patton. Is she all right?'

'May I see your license, please?'

'I don't have a license. I'm just learning to drive. I have a learner's permit. Is the woman all right?'

'May I see the permit, please?'

The officer should have known, but didn't, that in

I

this state, within many sections of the Vehicle and Traffic Law, a learner's permit was deemed a license to drive. All he knew was that here was a sobbing sixteen-year-old kid who'd just run over a woman who looked like she was maybe twenty-eight, twenty-nine years old.

They were standing outside the vehicle that had knocked her down, a blue Ford Escort with dual brake pedals and oversized yellow and black STUDENT DRIVER plates on the front and rear bumpers. The impact had sent the woman flying some five feet into the air, tossing her onto a pile of burning leaves stacked on the sidewalk near the curb. One of the witnesses had dragged her off the smoldering fire, onto the lawn, and had immediately called the police. Other blues at the scene were still searching for the handbag the witness said she'd been carrying. But the stricken woman was wearing red, and the leaves on the ground were thick this fall.

They kept scuffing through the fallen leaves, searching for the camouflaged bag, hoping to find a driver's license, a business card, a phone bill with a name and address on it – anything that would tell them who she was. Anonymous, she lay in the gutter some twenty feet from where a highway patrol car was just pulling in behind the Ford. Red coat open over a blue skirt and jacket, white blouse with a stock tie. Eyes closed. Hands at her sides, palms upward, fingers twitching.

The blues took the highway patrolmen aside and informed them that they'd tested the guy's skills and he'd failed with flying colors and seemed to be high on something. Nobody smelt alcohol but they gave him a breathalyzer test, anyway, and discovered no trace whatever of methyl alcohol in his system, the guy blew much lower than point-one-oh. One of them asked him his name, which the blues had already done. He still didn't know. Shook his head and almost fell off his feet. They opened the door on the passenger side of the Ford and let him sit.

'He's Mr Newell,' the girl said. 'He's been giving me driving lessons. I don't know how this happened, she just stepped off the curb. Oh my God, is she all right?'

'Can you tell us his first name?'

'Andrew. Will she be all right?'

The ambulance arrived along about then. It was almost three thirty. Paramedics lifted the woman onto a stretcher and hoisted her inside. The ambulance pulled away from the curb. Nobody yet knew who the woman was. The street seemed suddenly very still. A fresh wind sent withering leaves rattling along the curb.

'I think you'll both have to come along with us,' one of the blues said to the young blonde girl and the man who seemed stoned.

The girl nodded.

'Will you call my father, please?' she asked.

The phone was ringing when Katie got back to the apartment that afternoon. She put the two bags of groceries on the table just inside the door and went swiftly to the kitchen counter, sitting on one of the stools there and yanking the phone from its wall hook at the same time.

'Logan,' she said.

'Katie, it's Carl.'

'Yes, Carl.'

'Can you get down here right away? Lieutenant needs you to question a female juve.'

'Sure,' she said. 'Give me ten minutes.'

'See you,' Carl said, and hung up.

Katie sighed and put the phone back on its hook. This was supposed to be her day off. But she was the only woman detective in the department and whenever they got a young girl in, the job went to her. She was wearing, on this bright fall afternoon, a tan plaid skirt with low heels, opaque brown pantyhose and a matching brown sweater. The skirt was on the short side; she'd have to change before driving downtown. She'd also have to call Max again to see if there was any further word from her dear departed husband. Worst thing about a detective squadroom in a small town was the lack of privacy. River Close claimed a mere 50,000 inhabitants – well, some fifty-five during July and August, but all the summer renters were gone now.

She went to the kitchen window and cranked it open. A gust of cool air rushed into the apartment, carrying with it the aroma of woodsmoke. From the junior high school across the street, she could hear the sounds of football practice. Today was the sixteenth of October, a clear brisk day during one of the most glorious falls Katie could recall. Spoiled, of course. Autumn spoiled forever. Stephen had left her on the twelfth of September. Easy come, easy go, she thought. She'd only known him since she was sixteen.

Until now, she'd always thought of autumn as her time of year. Sometimes felt she even *looked* like autumn, the reddish-brown hair and freckled cheeks echoing the season's colors, her eyes as blue as any September sky. She'd hated the freckles when she was a little girl, but at thirty-three she felt they added character to her face. Made her look a bit more Irish, too, as if she needed any help with a name like Katherine Byrne Logan.

She wondered all at once if she should go back to her maiden name after the divorce. She was so used to being Katie Logan, so used to being Detective Logan, so used to being just plain *Logan* that . . .

Call Max, she thought.

She looked at the wall clock. Ten minutes to four. Better get cracking.

First the frozen stuff, she thought, and began unpacking the groceries.

5

Max Binder had been recommended to Katie by a lawyer she knew in the State Attorney's Office. A portly, avuncular man with white hair and chubby cheeks, he seemed uncommonly well-suited to the task of consoling forlorn women seeking divorces. Katie supposed she fell into this category. A forlorn woman. Deserted, desolate and forsaken. If she were any more Irish, she'd be keening. Instead, she was dialing the three B's and hoping Max wasn't in court.

'Binder, Benson and Byrd,' said a woman's voice.

'Ellie, it's Katie Logan,' she said. 'Is he in?'

'Second.'

Max came on the phone a moment later.

'Hi, Katie, what's new?' he asked.

Same question every time. What's new is my husband left me and is living with a twenty-two-year-old waitress is what's new.

'Have you heard from him?' she asked.

'Not yet.'

'What's taking him so long?'

'He only got our counter-proposal a week ago. You're being eminently fair, Katie. I can't imagine him refusing at this point.'

'Then call Schiffman and light a fire under him.'

'Schiffman's trying a big case this week.'

'Shall I call him myself?'

'Schiffman? No, no. No. No, Katie.'

'How about Stephen then? My alleged husband.'

'No. Certainly not.'

'I want a divorce, Max.'

'Of course you do. But be patient just a little longer, Katie. Please. I'm handling it. Please.'

'OK, Max.'

'OK, Katie? Please.'

'Sure,' she said. 'Let me know.'

She hung up and looked at the clock.

'On my way,' she said aloud.

Rebecca Patton's dark-brown eyes were shining with tears. Behind her, the high windows of the room framed trees bursting with leaves of red, orange, yellow and brown. They were sitting in what the local precinct had labeled the 'interrogation room', after those in big-city police departments, though normally the cops at Raleigh Station didn't put on airs. Katie hadn't yet told her that the woman she'd hit was in a critical condition at Gardner General Hospital. She hadn't yet told her that so far the woman hadn't been able to speak to anyone. Still anonymous, the hospital had admitted her as Jane Doe.

'Rebecca,' Katie said, 'your father just got here. If you'd like him to come in while we talk . . .'

'Yes, I would, please,' Rebecca said.

'And if your mother would like to join us . . .'

'My mother's in California.'

A sudden sharpness of voice which startled Katie.

7

'They're divorced.'

'I see.'

'I hope no one called her.'

'I really don't know. I'm assuming the –'

She almost said 'arresting officers'.

She caught herself.

'– responding officers called whoever...'

'I didn't give them her name. I don't want her to know about this.'

'If that's your wish.'

'It's my wish.'

'Let me get your father, then.'

Dr Ralph Patton was sitting on a bench in the corridor just outside the squadroom. He got to his feet the moment he saw Katie approaching. A tall spare man wearing blue jeans, a denim shirt, loafers and a suede vest, he looked more like a wrangler than a physician – but Wednesday was his day off. His dark-brown eyes were the color of his daughter's. They checked out the ID tag clipped to the pocket of Katie's gray tailored suit, and immediately clouded with suspicion.

'Where's Rebecca?' he asked.

'Waiting for us,' Katie said. 'She's fine, would you come with me, please?'

'What's she doing in a police station?'

'I thought you'd been informed...'

'Yes, the officer who called told me Rebecca was

8

involved in an automobile accident. I repeat. What's she doing here?'

'Well, there are questions we have to ask, Dr Patton, I'm sure you realize that. About the incident.'

'Why? Since when is an accident a crime?'

'We haven't charged her with any crime,' Katie said. Which was true.

But a young woman lay critically injured in the hospital, knocked down by the automobile Rebecca Patton had been driving. And the only licensed driver in the subject vehicle had been under the influence of something, they still didn't know what. If the woman died, Katie figured Andrew Newell was looking at either vehicular homicide or reckless manslaughter. But whereas the law considered the licensed driver to be primary, if the learner behind the wheel *knew* that he wasn't in complete control of all his faculties, they might *both* be culpable.

'Are we going to need a lawyer here?' Dr Patton asked, brown eyes narrowing suspiciously again.

'That's entirely up to you,' Katie said.

'Yes, I want one,' he said.

Technically, the girl was in police custody.

And in keeping with the guidelines, as a juvenile she was being questioned separately and apart from any criminals who might be on the premises, of whom there were none, at the moment, unless Andrew

Newell in the lieutenant's office down the hall could be considered a criminal for having abused whatever substance was in his body when he'd climbed into that Ford.

The Patton lawyer was here now, straight out of Charles Dickens, wearing mutton chops and a tweedy jacket and a bow tie and gold-rimmed spectacles and sporting a checkered vest and a little pot belly and calling himself Alexander Wickett.

'How long have you been driving?' Katie asked.

'Since the beginning of August,' Rebecca said.

'Does she have to answer these questions?' her father asked.

Wickett cleared his throat and looked startled.

'Why, no,' he said. 'Not if she doesn't wish to. You heard Miss Logan repeating Miranda in my presence.'

'Then why don't you advise her to remain silent?'

'Well, do you *wish* to remain silent, Miss Patton?'

'Did I hurt that woman?' Rebecca asked.

'Yes, you hurt her,' Katie said. 'Very badly.'

'Oh God.'

'She's in critical condition at Gardner General.'

'God, dear God.'

'Do you want to answer questions or don't you?' Dr Patton said.

'I want to help.'

'Answering questions won't—'

'However I can help, I want to. I didn't mean to hit

her. She stepped right off the curb. There was no way I could avoid her. I saw this flash of red and ... and ...'

'Becky, I think you should—'

'No. I want to help. Please.' She turned to Katie and said, 'Ask whatever you like, Miss Logan.'

Katie nodded.

'Do you consider yourself a good driver, Rebecca?'

'Yes. I was planning to take my test next week, in fact.'

'How fast were you going at the time of the accident?'

'Thirty miles an hour. That's the speed limit in that area.'

'You've been there before?'

'Yes. Many times. We drive all over the city. Main roads, back roads, all over. Mr Newell's a very good teacher. He exposes his students to all sorts of conditions. His theory is that good driving is knowing how to react instantly to any given circumstance.'

'So you've been on that street before?'

'Yes.'

'When did you first see the woman?'

'I told you. She stepped off the curb just as I was approaching the corner.'

'Did you slow down at the corner?'

'No. There are full stop signs on the cross street. Both sides of Grove. But Third is the through street. I wasn't supposed to slow down.'

'Did Mr Newell advise you to use caution at that particular corner?'

'No. Why would he?'

'Did *he* see the woman before you did?'

'I don't think so.'

'Well, did he say anything in warning?'

'No. What his system is, he asks his students to tell him everything they see. He'll say, "What do you see?" And you'll answer, "A milk truck pulling in," or "A girl on a bike," or "A red light," or "A car passing on my left," like that. He doesn't comment unless you *don't* see something. Then he'll say again, "What do you see *now*?" Emphasizing it. This way he knows everything going through our heads.'

'When you approached that corner, did he ask you what you were seeing?'

'No. In fact, he'd been very quiet. I thought I must have been driving exceptionally well. But it was a pretty quiet afternoon, anyway. No video games.'

'No what?'

'Video games. That's what he called unexpected situations. When everything erupts as if you're driving one of those cars in a video arcade? Six nuns on bicycles, a truck spinning out of control, a drunk staggering across the road. Video games.'

'Did you at any time suspect that Mr *Newell* might be drunk? Or under the influence of drugs?'

'Not until he got out of the car. After the accident.'

'What happened then?'

'Well, first off, he almost fell down. He grabbed the car for support and then started to walk towards the police officer, but he was weaving and ... and stumbling ... acting just like a drunk, you know, but I knew he couldn't be drunk.'

'How'd you know that?'

'Well, he wasn't drunk when we started the lesson, and he didn't have anything to drink while we were driving, so how could he be drunk?'

'But he couldn't even give the police his name, isn't that right?'

'Well, he could hardly talk at all. Just ... you know ... his speech was slurred, you could hardly understand him.'

'Was this the case while you were driving? During the lesson?'

'No.'

'He spoke clearly during the lesson?'

'Well, as I said, he didn't make very many comments. I think there were one or two times he asked me what I saw, and then he was quiet for the most part.'

'Was this unusual?'

'Well, no, actually. He never commented unless I was doing something wrong. Then he'd say, "What do you see?" Or sometimes, to test me, he'd *let* me go through a stop sign, for example, and then tell me about it afterward.'

'But this afternoon, there weren't many comments?'

'No.'

'He just sat there.'

'Well, yes.'

'Before the woman stepped off the curb, did he ask you what you saw?'

'No.'

'Did he hit the brake on his side of the car?'

'No.'

Andrew Newell didn't come out of it until eight forty-five that night.

Detective Second Grade Carl Williams sat on the edge of a desk in the lieutenant's office, and watched the man trying to shake the cobwebs loose from his head. Blinking into the room. Seeing Carl, blinking again. No doubt wondering where he was and who this big black dude was sitting on the edge of the desk.

'Mr Newell?'

'Mmm.'

'Andrew Newell?'

'Mmm.'

'What are you on, Mr Newell?'

'What?'

'What'd you take, sir, knocked you on your ass that way?'

Newell blinked again.

Go ahead, say it, Carl thought.

'Where am I?' Newell asked.

Bingo.

'Raleigh Station, River Close PD,' Carl said. 'What kind of controlled substance did you take, man?'

'Who the hell are you?'

'Carl Williams, Detective Second, pleased to meet you. Tell me what kind of drug you took, knocked you out that way.'

'I don't know what you're talking about.'

Good-looking white man sitting in the lieutenant's black leather chair, blondish going gray, pale eyes bloodshot after whatever it was he'd taken. Coming out of it almost completely now, looking around the room, realizing he was in some kind of police facility, the lieutenant's various trophies on his bookshelves, the framed headlines from the *River Close Herald* when Raleigh Station broke the big drug-smuggling case three years ago. Blinking again. Still wondering what this was all about. Tell him, Carl thought.

He told him.

'According to what we've got, you were giving Rebecca Patton a driving lesson this afternoon when she ran into a woman. We don't yet know her name. She's in critical condition at Gardner General. Car was equipped with dual brakes. You were the licensed driver in the vehicle, but you didn't hit the brake on your side of the car because you were too stoned either to see the woman stepping off the curb or to react in time to avoid the accident. Now I have to tell you seriously here, Mr Newell, that if the girl didn't know you were under the influence, if she had put her trust in you as her instructor and, in effect, you broke this trust, and this accident occurred, then most likely – and I'm not speaking for the State Attorney here – but most likely you would be the person considered culpable under the law. So it might be a good idea for you to tell me just when you took this drug, whatever it was, and why you knowingly got into a vehicle while under—'

'I didn't take any damn drug,' Newell said. 'I want a lawyer right this goddamn minute.'

Working in the dark on Grove Avenue, playing his flashlight over the leaves on the lawn and in the gutter, Joseph Bisogno kept searching for the red handbag he'd seen the woman carrying just before the car hit her. The police had given up finding it about a half-hour ago, but Joseph knew it was important to them, otherwise they wouldn't have been turning over every leaf in the neighborhood looking for it.

Joseph was sixty-eight years old, a retired steel worker from the days when River Close was still operating the mills and polluting the atmosphere. These days the mills were gone and the town's woman mayor had campaigned on a slogan of 'Clean Air, Clean Streets'. She was about Joseph's age. He admired her a great deal because she was doing something with her life. Joseph had the idea that if he found the handbag, he might become a key figure in this big case the police were working. Newspaper headlines. 'Retired Steelworker Key to Accident.' Television interviews. 'Tell us, Mr Bisogno, did you notice the woman *before* the car struck her?' 'Well, I'll tell you the truth, it all happened so fast...'

But, no, it hadn't happened that fast at all.

He'd been out front raking leaves when he saw the woman coming out of the church across the street, Our Lady of Sorrows, the church he himself attended every now and then when he was feeling particularly pious and holy, which was rarely. He enjoyed exercising out of doors, made him feel healthier than when he worked out on the bedroom treadmill. Mowing the lawn, picking weeds, raking leaves the way he'd been doing today, this kind of activity made him feel not like sixty-eight but forty-seven, which was anyway the age he thought of himself as being. Think of yourself as forty, then you'll feel like forty, his wife used to say. But that was before she got cancer.

He was willing to bet a thousand dollars that Mayor Rothstein thought of herself as forty-seven. Good-looking woman, too. Jewish woman. He liked Jewish women – had dated a Jewish girl named Hedda Gold when he was seventeen; she certainly knew how to kiss. Mayor Rothstein had hair as black as Tessie's hair had been before she passed away seven years ago. Maybe if he found the handbag, the mayor would ask him to head up a committee, give him something to do with his life other than mourning Tessie all the time – poor, dear Tessie.

The woman had come down the church steps, red coat flapping open in a mild autumn breeze, red handbag to match, blue skirt and white blouse under it, blue jacket, head bent as if she had serious thoughts on her mind. Leaves falling everywhere around her. Coins from heaven, Tessie used to say. He wondered if Mayor Rothstein believed in heaven; he certainly didn't. Next door, his neighbor had already started a small fire of leaves at the curb. Woman coming up the path from the church now, turning left where the path joined the sidewalk, coming toward where Joseph, on the other side of the street, was raking his leaves.

He thought...

For a moment, he thought the car was slowing down because the driver had seen the woman approaching the curb. A blue Ford, coming into the street slowly, cautiously. But then he realized this was a beginning driver, big yellow and black plate on the front bumper, STUDENT DRIVER, the woman stepping off the curb unheedingly, head still bent, the car speeding up as if the driver hadn't seen her after all. And then, oh

God, he almost yelled to the woman, almost shouted, *Watch* it! The car, the woman, they ... he *did* shout this time; yelled 'Lady!' at the top of his lungs, but it was too late. The car hit her with a terrible wrenching thud, metal against flesh, and the woman went up into the air, legs flying, arms flying, the collision throwing her onto his neighbor's leaf fire at the curb, the shrieking of brakes, the driver leaning on her horn too late, too late, all of it too late.

The girl driving the car did not get out.

Neither did the man sitting beside her.

The girl put her head on the steering wheel, not looking at Joseph as he dragged the woman off the fire and rolled her onto the lawn. Joseph went inside to call the police. When he came out again, the girl still had her head on the wheel. The woman's red coat was charred where the flames had got to it.

He remembered all of it now.

Visualized it all over again. The woman going up into the air, legs and arms wide, as if she were trying to fly, arms going up into the air...

The handbag.

Yes.

Flying out of her hands, going up, up...

He suddenly knew where it was.

Newell's attorney didn't get to Raleigh Station until almost ten o'clock that night. His name was Martin

Leipman; a smart young man Carl had met on several prior occasions, usually while testifying in court. He was wearing a shadow-striped black suit with a white shirt and a maroon tie that looked like a splash of coagulated blood. He had no objection to Carl reading Miranda to his client – as why would he? – and he listened silently while Carl ascertained that Newell had understood everything he'd explained, and was ready to proceed with answering the questions put to him. Since this had got so serious all of a sudden, Carl had also requested a police stenographer to record whatever Newell might have to say about the accident.

'You understand we can call this off anytime you say, don't you?' Leipman asked him.

'I do,' Newell said.

'Just so you know. Go ahead, Detective.'

Carl said, 'Do you remember anything that happened on Grove and Third this afternoon?'

'No, I don't,' Newell said.

'You don't remember the automobile striking that woman?'

'I don't.'

'You don't remember the responding police officers asking you your name?'

'No, I don't.'

'Do you remember taking any drug that would have put you in this altered state?'

'No.'

'Tell me what you do remember?'

'Starting when?'

'Starting when you got into that car.'

'That was after school. I teach Art Appreciation at Buckley High, and I give driving lessons after classes, twice a week. Rebecca Patton is one of my students. She had a lesson today, at ten minutes to three. I don't know who's on the schedule until I see the chart posted in the Driver's Ed office. I go there after my last class, look at the chart and then go out to the trainer car. I was waiting in the Ford at a quarter to three, behind the area where the busses pull in. She knew where to go. She began taking lessons with me over the summer vacation, started at the beginning of August actually...'

... actually, he's known Rebecca since the term before, when she and her father moved from Washington, D.C. to River Close. Art Appreciation is what is known as a crap course at Buckley High, a *snap* course if one wishes to be politically correct, but Rebecca takes it more seriously than many of the other students do, going to the public library on her own to take out books on the old masters, copying pictures from them by hand...

'I'm certain she would have gone to a museum if River Close had one, but of course we don't...'

... so the library had to suffice. She brings her drawings in every week – the class meets only once a week – and asks specific questions about composition and perspective, and color and design, but especially about tension, playing back to him his theory that all works of art are premised on the tension the artist generates within the prescribed confines of the canvas, the painting tugging at the frame in all directions to provide the thrill a spectator feels in the presence of genius.

'I got to know her a little better in August,' Newell said, 'when we began the driving lessons. She told me she wanted to do something creative with her life. She didn't know quite what, whether it'd be music, or art, or even writing, but *something*. She'd just turned sixteen, but she already knew that she didn't plan to spend her life as a bank teller or a telephone operator, she had to do something that required imagination. She told me I'd been responsible for that. My class. What I taught in my class.'

'How'd you feel about that, Mr Newell?' Carl asked.

'I was flattered. And I felt ... well, that I'd done my job. I'd inspired a young mind to think creatively. That's important to me. When I'm teaching art, I always ask my students "What do you see?" I want them to scrutinize any given painting and tell me in detail what they're seeing. That's how I forge a link between my students and the artist, by asking them to actually *see* what the artist saw while he was executing the work. I try to expand their horizons. I teach them to dare. I teach them to . . .'

'Let's get back to this afternoon, shall we?' Carl said.

'We've already covered this afternoon,' Leipman said. 'Unless you've got something new to add.'

'Counselor, I still don't know what your client took.'

'I told you . . .'

'He told you . . .'

'Then how'd he get in the condition he was in?'

A knock sounded discreetly on the door.

'Come in,' Carl said.

Johnny Bicks, the third man on the squad's afternoon shift, poked his head around the door. 'Talk to you a minute?' he asked.

'Sure,' Carl said, and went out into the hall with him.

'Some guy just came in with what he claims is the victim's handbag,' Johnny said.

'Where is he?'

'Downstairs, at the desk. I already told Katie.'

'Thanks,' Carl said. He opened the door to the lieutenant's office, leaned into the room and said, 'Excuse me a moment, I'll be right back,' and then closed the door and headed for the steps leading downstairs.

The man standing with Katie at the muster desk was telling her that he'd found the bag in one of the trees

23

on Frank Pollack's lawn; his neighbor's lawn. Caught in like one of those forks in the branches, you know? Hard to see because it was red and so were the leaves all around it. Besides, the police officers had been searching the *ground*, you know? Nobody had thought to look up in the trees.

Katie asked the desk sergeant if he had any gloves back there, and he reached under the desk and handed her a pair of somewhat filthy white cotton gloves that had been used in accepting evidence two or three times before, she guessed. As she pulled on the gloves, she realized Mr Bisogno here had already handled the bag but no sense adding insult to injury.

'How do you know it's the victim's?' Carl asked.

'I saw her carrying it,' Bisogno said. 'I'm the one told the officers she was carrying a red handbag.'

Katie was reaching into the bag for the woman's wallet.

'You witnessed the accident?' Carl asked.

'I did.'

Katie opened the wallet.

The phone on the muster desk was ringing.

'Raleigh Station, Sergeant Peters.'

Katie pulled out the woman's driver's license.

'Just a second,' Peters said. 'Katie, for you. It's somebody at Gardner General.'

She took the phone.

'Detective Logan,' she said.

'This is Dr Hagstrom in the Emergency Room at Gardner,' a man's voice said.

'Yes, Dr Hagstrom?'

'The Jane Doe we received at three fifty this afternoon?'

'Yes?'

'She's dead,' Hagstrom said.

'Thank you,' Katie said, and handed the phone back to Peters. 'We've got a homicide,' she told Carl.

Carl nodded.

Katie looked at the license in her hand.

The name on it was Mary Beth Newell.

The State Attorney who came to Raleigh Station that night at twenty to eleven was dressed in blue tailored slacks and jacket, no blouse under it, a Kelly green silk scarf at her throat picking up the virtually invisible shadow stripe of the suit. Alyce Hart was wearing blue French-heeled shoes as well, no earrings, no make-up except lipstick. Her brown hair was cut in a wedge that gave a swift look to her angular face, as if she were a schooner cutting through the wind. Katie liked everything about her but the way she chose to spell her first name. Carl liked her because he felt she thought like a man, which Alyce might have considered a dubious compliment. The three of them had worked together before; this was a small town.

'Breathalyzer was negative, right?' she asked.

'Yeah,' Carl said.

'So what was he on?'

'Who knows?'

'Whatever it was, he's wide awake now,' Katie said.

'Can we do a blood test?' Carl asked.

'Under Miranda, you mean?' Alyce said.

'Yeah.'

'Not without his consent. Nothing I'd like better than to see what kind of juice is running through his veins, have him pee for us, too. But we'd need a court order for that, and we can't get one till he's arraigned. This was New York, Chicago, any other big bad city, we'd find an open court, have him arraigned tonight. River Close, though, just *try* to wake up some judge this hour of the night. We'll be lucky if he's arraigned by two, three tomorrow afternoon.'

'Which may be too late,' Katie said.

'Depending on what kind of shit he took,' Carl said.

'If we can't show he was on *something*,' Alyce said, 'we've got no case.'

'Well, we've got witnesses at the scene,' Carl said.

'The girl's a witness, too,' Katie said.

'Sure, but Newell's attorney might...'

'No question,' Carl said.

'Right, claim he...'

'You can bet the farm on it,' Alyce said. 'He'll say the *accident* caused it. Shock, whatever. Couldn't walk, couldn't talk, couldn't remember his own name.

Anyway, let's charge him and hold him. We may be able to get an early-morning arraignment. If not, we pray it was a drug with a long half-life. You agree with vehicular manslaughter?'

'I wish we could go for reckless,' Carl said. 'Guy pops pills, and then knowingly gets in a car with a *learner*? He's not only risking *her* life, he's courting disaster with everybody on the street.'

'Let me offer the grand jury a choice,' Alyce said. 'Shoot for reckless manslaughter, settle for vehicular. How does that sound?'

'Good to me,' Katie said.

'Me, too,' Carl said.

'Let's get some sleep,' Alyce said.

Don't let the bimbo answer, Katie thought.

She was sitting at the kitchen counter, sipping a Scotch and soda. The clock on the wall read three minutes to midnight. The phone kept ringing. Three, four, not the bimbo, she prayed.

'Hello?'

The bimbo.

'Let me talk to Stephen, please,' she said.

'Who's this?'

'Mrs Logan,' she said.

'His mother?'

Sure, his mother, Katie thought.

Who happens to be dead.

'His *wife*,' she said, hitting the word hard.

'Oh.'

Long pause.

'Just a sec, OK?'

Sounding like a teeny bopper. Twenty-two years old, Katie thought. The minute hand on the wall clock lurched. Eleven fifty-eight. My how the time flies when you're having...

'Hello?'

'Stephen?'

'Yes?'

'Katie.'

'Yes, Katie. Do you know what time it is?'

'I spoke to my attorney today...'

'Katie, we're not supposed to be doing this.'

'Doing what?'

'Talking. The attorneys are supposed to do all the talking.'

'Oh dear, am I breaking the law?' she asked.

'You know you're not breaking the law. But...'

'Then hear me out. We sent you a counter-proposal last week, and we haven't yet heard from you. I'm eager to get on with this, Stephen. I thought you were, too. Instead...'

'I am.'

'That's what I imagined. You're the one who left, Stephen.'

'Katie, I really think we should let the lawyers

handle this, is what I think, really.'

'I really think you should tell me what's taking you so long to study a one-page document, is what *I* think, really.'

'Katie . . .' he said.

And hesitated.

She waited.

'Give me a little time, OK?' he said softly. 'Please.'

And all at once she was bewildered.

In bed that night, all night long, she kept remembering. Because, honestly, you know, she'd had no clue. Smart cop, first in her class at the academy, promoted to detective after a year on the force when she'd walked into a silent-alarm holdup and apprehended two guys twice her size who were wanted for armed robbery in Indiana, a hell of a long way away, but who was measuring? Smart detective. Had no clue at all that Stephen was cheating on her.

Well, married to the same guy for ten years, who would have guessed? Such a lovely couple, everyone said. High-school sweethearts, everyone said. She'd waited for him while he was in the army, waited for him when he was called up again and sent to yet another distant nation. There was always something to defend, she guessed, honor or oil or some damn thing. But, oh, how handsome he'd looked on the day they were married, Captain Stephen Gregory Logan, in his dress uniform, Miss Katharine Kyle Byrne, all in white, though certainly no virgin. Well, high-school sweethearts, you know. Met him when she was sixteen.

Who would have guessed? Not a clue.

There were the hours, of course.

A policeman's lot is not a happy one, the man once wrote and he'd been right. The graveyard shift was the worst. You wouldn't think there'd be much crime in a small city like River Close but there were drugs everywhere in America these days, and drugs moved day and night, so you had to have round the clock shifts, and you had to have cops who caught those shifts, on rotation, every three months. Whenever she jammed what was officially called 'the morning shift', Katie left for work at eleven fifteen to get to the squadroom at a quarter to midnight, and didn't get home till a quarter past eight, by which time Stephen had already left for work. During those three months, she saw him maybe five, six hours a day. That wasn't too good for the marriage, she realized now, but who would have guessed then? They're so much in love, everyone said.

So last month, she gets home from a long hard afternoon shift, four to midnight, gets home at about a quarter to one in the morning, and he's sitting in his pajamas in the living room, the lights out, a drink in his hand, and he tells her he's leaving.

Leaving? she says.

She doesn't know what he means at first. Well, the thought is inconceivable, really. His job doesn't call for travel, he's never been *sent* anywhere in all the years of their marriage, so what does he mean, he's leaving? He's a vice president at the bank. In fact it was *his* bank the two hoods from Indiana were trying to rob that day she caught the squeal, away back then when she was twenty-five and riding shotgun in a patrol car with Carl Williams. She always kidded Stephen that he got his promotion to vice president only because she thwarted the hold-up. So what does he mean, he's leaving?

You, he says. I'm leaving you.

Come on, she says, I had a hard day.

Irish sense of humor, right?

Wrong.

He was leaving her.

The police had confiscated the training vehicle the school used for its Driver's Ed course. Technicians from the lab had searched it for evidence that Newell – as instructor and supervisor – had, in effect, been 'driving' the car in violation of subdivision four of section 1192 of the Vehicle and Traffic Law, which stated: 'No person shall operate a motor vehicle while the person's ability to operate such a vehicle is impaired by the use of a drug as defined in this chapter.'

The drugs referred to were listed in the Public Health Law and constituted a virtual pharmacology of every opiate, opium derivative, hallucinogenic substance and stimulant known to man. And woman, too, Katie thought.

On Thursday morning, the day after the fatal accident, they drove over to Our Lady of Sorrows in one of the Pontiac sedans set aside for the Raleigh Station's detectives. Carl was driving, Katie was riding shotgun beside him.

'Guess what Annie cooked again last night?' Carl asked.

'Asparagus,' Katie said.

'Asparagus,' Carl said. 'We're married six years, she *knows* I hate asparagus, but she keeps making asparagus. I told her why do you keep making asparagus when you know I hate it? First she says, "It's good for you." I tell her I don't *care* if it's good for me, I don't like the taste of it. So she says, "You'll *get* to like the taste of it." So I tell her I'm thirty-seven years old, I've been hating asparagus for thirty-seven years, I am *never* going to like the taste of it. You know what she says next?'

'What?' Katie asked.

'She says, "Anyway, you *do* like it." Can you believe that? I'm telling her I hate it, she tells me I like it. So I tell her one more time I *hate* asparagus, please don't make asparagus again, I *hate* it! So she says, "When

you get to be President of the United States, you won't
have to eat asparagus. Meanwhile, it's good for you." '

'That was broccoli.'

'Just what I told her.'

'There's the church,' Katie said.

Bright morning sunlight was flooding the churchyard
as they entered it through an arched wooden door
leading from the church proper. Katie had expected to
find Father McDowell on his knees in prayer. Saying
matins, she imagined, wasn't that the one they said in
the morning? The good father was, in fact, on his
knees – but he was merely gathering flowers. Katie
guessed he was a man in his early seventies, with a
ruddy face which led her to believe he enjoyed a touch
of the sacrificial wine every now and again. He greeted
them warmly and told them at once that he himself had
planted the mums he was now cutting for the altar.
Planned the garden so that it bloomed all through the
spring, summer and autumn months. The mums he
was carefully placing in a wicker basket were yellow
and white and purple and brown. They reminded Katie
of Stephen, damn him! Excuse me, father, she thought.

'We're here to ask about a woman named Mary Beth
Newell,' she said. 'We have reason to believe she was
here at Our Lady of Sorrows yesterday. Would you
remember her?'

'Yes, of course,' McDowell said.

He snipped another stem, carefully placing stem and bloom alongside the others in the basket.

A football game. Stephen bringing Katie a bright orange mum to pin to her white cheerleader's sweater. The big letter B on the front of the sweater. For Buckley High.

'Is it true her husband has been arrested for killing her?' McDowell asked.

'He's been charged with vehicular homicide, yes, Father.'

'But why? I understand a young girl was driving.'

'That's true. But he was the licensed driver.'

'It still seems...'

'The girl didn't know he was under the influence. State attorney believes the fault was his. *Did* Mrs Newell come here yesterday?'

'She did.'

'Can you tell us what time she got here?'

'Around two fifteen, two twenty.'

'And left when?'

'An hour or so later.'

They were here to learn whether or not the priest had seen the accident. They were building a list of reliable witnesses, the more the merrier. But McDowell's response stopped Katie cold. Her next question should have been, 'Did you see her leaving the church?' Instead, she said, 'Mrs Newell spent a full *hour* with you?'

'Well, almost, yes.'

Katie suddenly wondered why.

'Father,' she said, 'we know Mrs Newell lived in St Matthew's parish, some ten blocks from here.'

'That's right.'

'Is that where she worships?'

'I have no idea.'

'Well, does she worship here?'

'No, she doesn't.'

'Then what was she doing here, Father?'

'She'd been coming to me for spiritual guidance.'

'Are you saying that today wasn't the *only* time she...?'

'I can't tell you anything more, I'm sorry.'

Katie knew all about privileged communication, thanks. But she was Irish. And she sniffed something in the wind.

'Father,' she said, 'no one's trying to pry from you whatever...'

McDowell was Irish, too.

'I'm sorry,' he said, and snipped another stem as though he were decapitating someone possessed by the devil. Katie figured he was signaling an end to the conversation. Gee, Father, tough, she thought.

'Father,' she said, 'we don't want to know *what* you talked about...' Like hell we don't, she thought. '... but if you can tell us when she first came to see you.'

'Is that why you're here?' McDowell said. 'To invade a dead woman's privacy?' Wagging his head scornfully, he rose from where he was kneeling, almost losing his balance for a moment, but regaining it at once, his prized basket of cut flowers looped over his arm. Standing, he seemed to be at least six-feet tall. 'She got here at around two fifteen,' he repeated, 'and left about an hour later. Does that help you?'

'Sure, but when's the *first* time she came here?' Carl asked.

He'd been silent until now, letting Katie carry the ball. But sometimes a little muscle helped. Unless you were dealing with a higher authority. Like God.

'I'm sorry, I can't tell you that,' McDowell said.

So they double-ganged him.

'Did she spend an hour *each* time she visited you?' Katie asked.

'How many times *did* she visit, anyway?' Carl asked.

McDowell shook his head in disbelief. He was striding swiftly toward the entrance to the church now, the basket of flowers on his arm, the black skirts of his cassock swirling about his black trousers and highly polished black shoes. They kept pace with him, one on either side.

'She wasn't here to discuss her *husband*, was she?' Carl asked.

'Some problem her *husband* had?' Katie asked.

'Like a *drug* problem?' Carl asked.

McDowell stopped dead in his tracks. Pulling himself up to his full height, he said with dignity, 'The only problems Mary Beth discussed with me were her own. Good day, detectives.'

And went into his church.

So now they knew that Mary Beth Newell had problems.

Just before noon, Alyce Hart called the squadroom to say that Newell still hadn't been arraigned and if there were any further questions they wanted to ask, they'd best do it now. 'The irony of our judicial system,' she said, 'is that we can ask the accused anything we want *before* he's arraigned, but after that we need his lawyer's permission to talk to him.'

Katie wasn't quite sure what 'irony' meant, exactly. Besides, she couldn't think of anything she wanted to ask except what kind of dope Newell had taken and when he'd taken it.

At a quarter past one, the phone on her desk rang again. She picked up, identified herself, and listened as a member of the search team told her that the steering wheel had yielded no evidence that Rebecca Patton had, in fact, been driving the car when it hit Mary Beth Newell. Any prints on the wheel were hopelessly overlayed and smeared because too damn many students used the same training vehicle. The techs had also found palm and fingerprints on the driver's side dashboard, presumably left there by the several instructors who used the same car and who'd reached out protectively and defensively whenever a student's reaction time was a bit off. But these, too, were smeared or superimposed one upon the other, and did nothing to prove that Andrew Newell was effectively unconscious at the time of the accident.

Katie kept listening.

The next thing he said puzzled her.

At first she thought he'd said they'd found *cocaine* in the car. She *thought* he'd said, 'We also found a cup with a little *coke* in it.' Which was what he *had* said, but at the same time *hadn't* said.

A moment later, she learned that what he'd *actually* said was, 'We also found a cup with a little *Coke* in it.' Coke with a capital C. Coca *Cola* was what he was telling her. In the Ford's center console cup holder on the passenger side, they had found a medium-sized plastic cup with the red and white Coca Cola logo on it, which cup they had immediately tested.

Katie held her breath.

'Nothing but Coca Cola in it,' the tech said. 'But the guy sitting there could have used it to wash down whatever shit he ingested. A possibility, Kate.'

But . . .

He didn't have anything to drink while we were driving, so how could he be drunk?

How indeed? Katie wondered.

Katie got to the school at two twenty that afternoon. She went directly to the general office, showed a twenty-year-old brunette her shield and ID card, and asked for a copy of Rebecca Patton's program. The girl hesitated.

'Something wrong?' Katie asked.

'Nothing,' the girl said, and went to the files.

Katie waited while she photocopied the program. It told her that Rebecca would be in an eighth-period French class till the end of the school day.

'Where's the Driver's Ed office?' she asked.

'What do you need *there*?' the girl asked.

Katie looked at her.

'Down the hall,' the girl said at once, 'second door on the left. You're trying to send Mr Newell to jail, aren't you?'

'Yes,' Katie said, and walked out.

What she needed in the Driver's Ed office was a feel of the place. This was where Andrew Newell came at the end of each school day to consult the chart that told him which student would be driving that day. This was where he'd come yesterday, before getting into the car that would run down his wife. Here was the wall. Here was the chart. Here were the teachers' names and the students' names. Was this the room in which he'd ingested the drug – whichever the hell drug it was – that had, minutes later, rendered him incompetent?

'You're the detective, aren't you?' a man's voice said.

Katie turned from the wall chart.

'Saw you on television last night.' He was sprawled in an easy chair, open newspaper on his lap. 'Right after Andy was charged,' he said. 'Eleven o'clock news. The red hair,' he explained.

Katie nodded.

'Ed Harris,' he said. 'No relation.'

She must have looked puzzled.

'The movie star,' he said. 'Ed Harris. Besides, he's bald.'

This Ed Harris was not bald. He had thick black hair, graying at the temples, brown eyes behind dark-rimmed eyeglasses. He rose and extended his hand. Katie guessed he was half an inch short of six feet. Forty, forty-two, or thereabouts. Lean and lanky, like Abe Lincoln. Same rangy look. She took his hand.

'Are you going to send Andy to jail for the rest of his life?'

'Hardly,' she said, and almost shook her head in wonder. Their case was premised on the presumption that Newell had knowingly entered the training car while under the influence of a drug that had rendered him incapable of performing in his supervisory capacity. This constituted a criminally negligent act which had caused the death of another person. But the penalty for vehicular manslaughter in the second degree was only imprisonment not to exceed seven years. 'If he's found guilty,' she said, 'the maximum...'

'I sincerely hope he won't be.'

'Well, *if* he's convicted, the maximum sentence would be seven years. He could be out in two and a third.'

'Piece of cake, right?'

Katie said nothing.

'Two and a third *days* would destroy him,' Harris said.

She was thinking, If you can't do the time, don't do the crime. She still said nothing.

'For a lousy accident, right?' Harris said. 'Accidents *do* happen, you know.'

'Especially if a person's under the influence.'

'Andy doesn't drink.'

'Ever see him stoned?'

'Andy? Come on. If you knew him, you'd realize how ridiculous that sounds.'

'I take it you're good friends.'

'*Very* good friends.'

'Do you know Rebecca, too?'

'Sure, she's in my algebra class.'

'Is she a good student?'

'One of the best. Smart as hell, curious, eager to

learn. And from what Andy tells me, a good driver, too.'

'Not good enough. That's why there's a brake pedal on the instructor's side of the car.'

'Let me tell you something,' Harris said, and immediately looked up at the wall clock. She had seen his name on the chart for a driving lesson at two fifty with a student named Alberico Jiminez. The clock now read two thirty-five. In five minutes, Rebecca would be coming out of her French class. Katie didn't want to miss her.

'Andy and I both teach Driver's Ed,' Harris said. 'The classes are two hours long, twice a week. I teach them on Mondays and Thursdays, Andy teaches them on Wednesdays and Fridays. This is class time, you understand, not road time. Four hours a week. We try to teach *responsible* driving, Miss Logan, and we spend a great deal of time on how substance abuse affects ability and perception. These are teenagers, you know. Some of them drink, some of them smoke dope. We're all aware of that. Rebecca would have known in a minute if Andy had been under the influence. She knows all the signs, we've been over them a hundred times.'

'We have witnesses who saw him staggering, saw him—'

'Your witnesses are wrong.'

'My witnesses are police officers.'

Harris gave her a look.

'Right,' Katie said, 'we're out to frame the entire nation.'

'Nobody said that. But you know, Miss Logan...'

'Newell *should* have hit the brake. The responsibility was his.'

'No. If anyone was responsible, it was Mary Beth. She's the one who wasn't looking where she was going. She's the one who stepped off that curb and into the car.'

'How can you possibly know *what* she did?'

'I read the papers, I watch television. There were witnesses besides your police officers.'

'And she was your friend...'

'She was.'

'Any idea what might have been troubling her?'

'Who says she was troubled?'

'You didn't detect anything wrong?'

'No. Wrong? No.'

A bell sounded, piercing, insistent, reminding her that this was, in fact, a school, and that she was here to see a student.

As she turned to leave, Harris said, 'You're making a mistake here, Miss Logan. If nobody hit that brake, there simply wasn't *time* to hit it.'

'Good talking to you, Mr Harris,' Katie said.

'Ed,' he said. 'Don't hurt him.'

*

Rebecca came down the front steps of the school at a quarter to three, her books hugged to the front of her pale-blue sweater. Girls and boys were streaming down the steps everywhere around her, flowing toward where the idling yellow school busses were parked. A bright buzz of conversation, a warm consonance of laughter floated on the crisp October air.

'Hey, hi,' she said, surprised.

'Hi, Rebecca. Give you a ride home?'

'Well ... sure,' she said.

Katie fell into step beside her. Together, they walked in silence across the curving drive and into the parking lot. Leaves were falling everywhere around them, blowing on the wind, rustling underfoot. Katie reached into her tote bag. Her keys were resting beside the walnut stock of a .38 caliber Detectives Special. She dug them out and unlocked the door of the car on the passenger side.

'I sometimes think I'll never get in another car again,' Rebecca said.

'It wasn't your fault,' Katie said.

'It wasn't his, either.'

'Tell me something. When you said...'

'I don't want to say anything that will hurt Mr Newell.'

'His negligence killed someone,' Katie said flatly.

'You don't know he was drugged. Maybe he had a stroke or something. Or a heart attack. Something. It didn't have to be drugs. You just don't know for sure.'

'That's what we're trying to find out.'

'He must be *heart*broken, his own *wife*!'

'It doesn't matter who it was, he—'

'*I* was the one driving! Why should Mr Newell...?'

'You were in his custody.'

'I was *driving*!'

'And he was *stoned*!' Katie said sharply. 'His responsibility was to —'

'Please, please, don't.'

'Rebecca, listen to me!'

'What?'

Her voice catching. She's going to start crying again, Katie thought.

'Did you know he was drugged?' she asked.

'No.'

'Then you're not culpable, can you understand that? And protecting him would be a horrible mistake. I want you to answer one question.'

'I can't, please, I –'

'You *can*, damn it!'

Her voice crushed the autumn stillness. Leaves fell like colored shards of broken glass. In the distance there was the rumble of the big yellow busses pulling away from the school.

'You told me Andrew Newell didn't drink anything while you were driving,' Katie said. 'Is that still your recollection?'

Silence.

'Rebecca?'

The girl hugged her schoolbooks to her chest, head bent, blonde hair cascading on either side of her face. The sounds of the busses faded. Leaves fell, twisted, floated. They stood silently, side by side, in a stained-glass cathedral of shattered leaves. Gray woodsmoke drifted on the air from somewhere, everywhere. Katie suddenly remembered all the autumns there ever were.

'We stopped for a Coke,' Rebecca said.

'This was right after the lesson began,' Katie told Carl. They were sitting side by side at wooden desks in the squadroom. Most of the furniture here went back to the early forties when River Close first established a detective division. Until that time, any big case here, the chief had to call in detectives from the county seat up Twin River Junction. 'Say five after three; Rebecca didn't check her watch. Newell said he was thirsty, and directed her to the drive-in on Olive and High. They ordered a Coke for him at the drive-in window, and were on their way in five seconds flat. Newell kept sipping the Coke as they drove.'

'Did Rebecca see him popping any pills?'

'No.'

'So all we've got is the tech's guess.'

'Plus Newell stoned at the scene some fifteen minutes later.'

Both of them fell silent.

At four this afternoon, Newell had finally been arraigned, and they'd got their court order for blood and urine tests. They were waiting for the results now. Meanwhile, they had statements from all the various witnesses, but that was all they had.

It was now a quarter past five and dusk was coming on fast.

At six thirty, just as Katie and Carl were packing it in, the phone on her desk rang. It was Alyce Hart, calling to say that Newell's blood had tested positive for secobarbital sodium.

'Brand name's Seconal,' she said. 'Not often prescribed as a sedative these days. From what the lab tells me, fifty milligrams is the sedative dose. For Newell to have presented the effects he did at the scene, he had to've ingested at least three times that amount.'

'A hundred and fifty mills.'

'Right. That's the hypnotic dose for a man of his weight. Full hypnotic effect of the drug usually occurs fifteen to thirty minutes following oral or rectal administration.'

'Think somebody shoved it up his ass?'

'Unlikely. Effects would've been very similar to

alcoholic inebriation. Imperfect articulation of speech, failure of muscular coordination, clouded sensorium.'

'What's that?'

'Sensorium? State of consciousness or mental awareness. I had to ask, too.'

Which was another thing Katie liked about Alyce.

'How long would these effects last?' she asked.

'Three to eight hours.'

'Fits Newell, doesn't it?'

'Oh, doesn't it just?'

'Think he was an habitual user?'

'Who cares? We've got a case now, Katie.'

'We've also got what he washed the pills down with.'

'Oh?'

Katie told her about Newell stopping to buy a Coke just before the accident. She also mentioned that she'd been to Our Lady of Sorrows and had learned that Mary Beth Newell had taken her problems to the priest there, seeking spiritual guidance.

'Problems. What kind of problems?'

'He wouldn't say. But Our Lady of Sorrows isn't her parish.'

'What is her parish?'

'St Matthew's.'

'How far away?'

'Ten blocks.'

'Mm,' Alyce said, and was silent for a moment. 'What are you thinking, Katie?'

'Well . . . if Newell *knew* his wife was troubled about something, his lawyers might claim her state of mind was such that she caused the accident herself.'

'Yeah, go ahead.'

'By not paying attention to where she was going. Or even by deliberately stepping into the car's path.'

'It's a defense, yes,' Alyce said thoughtfully.

'So, what I was thinking is maybe we should try to find out exactly *what* was bothering her. Before the defense does. In fact, I thought I might drop in on her sister tomorrow morning.'

'OK, but don't expect too much. This may turn out to be nothing. Everybody has problems, Katie. Don't you have problems?'

'Me?' Katie said. 'Not a worry in the world.'

Thing she used to do when she and Stephen were still a proper man and wife, would be to ask him questions. 'Stephen, what does "irony" mean, exactly?' And, of course, he would tell her. He'd been telling her things ever since she was sixteen. Anything she wanted to know, she'd ask Stephen and he would tell her. So what she wanted to do *now* was pick up the phone and call him. Say, 'Hi, Stephen, I hope I'm not interrupting you and your bimbo at . . . what time is it, anyway? My oh my, is it *really* one fifteen in the morning? I certainly hope I'm not intruding. But someone used the word "irony" in my presence, and it occurred to me that although I often use that word myself, or even its sister word "ironic" I've never been really quite sure what *either* of those words mean exactly. So, Stephen, if it's not too much trouble, I wonder...'

But no.

Because you see, she and Stephen were no longer proper man and wife, she and Stephen were separated, that was the irony of it, that was what was so very damn ironic about the situation. So she got out of bed in her pajamas and padded barefoot to the little room Stephen had used as a study when he still lived here, and went to the bookshelves behind what used to be his desk and found the dictionary and thumbed through it till first she found 'iron' and then 'ironclad' and 'iron hand' and finally, bingo, there it was, 'ironic'. And guess what the definition was? The definition, according to Mr Webster himself, was: 'meaning the contrary of what is expressed.'

Huh? she thought.

How does that...?

She ran her finger down the page and found the word 'irony', and its first definition seemed to echo what she'd just learned about 'ironic'. In which case, she wondered, what's so damn *ironic* about them not being able to question Newell after he was arraigned? But hold it, kiddies, not so fast, here came the *second* definition. Katie took a sip of Scotch. 'Irony,' she read out loud. 'A result that is the opposite of what might be expected or considered appropriate.'

So if you can question a man because you *hope* to charge him with a crime, but then you can no longer question him after he's been *charged* with that crime, she guessed that was sure enough ironic.

Yep, that's irony, she thought.

How about that, Stephen?

How about that, hon?

A fine Friday-morning mist burnt away as Katie drove through the small village of River Bend, and then into the countryside again, where narrow streams wound through glades covered with fallen leaves. She drove onto a covered bridge, the interior of her car going dark, brilliant sunlight splashing her windshield a moment later. She hoped she wouldn't get a migraine, sudden changes of light often brought them on. Stephen would fetch her two aspirin tablets and advise her to lie down at once. No migraine, please, she thought. Not now. No Stephen to offer solace, you see.

The towns, hamlets, villages and occasional city in this part of the state suffered from a watery sameness of nomenclature due to a natural abundance of rivers and lakes. Mary Beth Newell's sister was a kindergarten teacher in Scotts Falls, named after the rapids that cascaded from the southernmost end of Lake Paskonomee, some twenty miles north-east of River Close, and within shouting distance of Twin River Junction, the county seat. If Andrew Newell had been charged with reckless endangerment, his attorney most likely would have asked for a change of venue and Alyce would have had to prosecute in Twin River J, as the town was familiarly known to the locals. Even with the lesser charge, Leipman might ask that the case be moved out of River Close. Either way, Alyce would go for the jugular.

Katie found Helen Pierce in a fenced-in area behind the elementary school. Katie had spoken to her only once before, on the telephone the night they learned Mary Beth Newell was dead. She had seen only police photographs of the dead woman's body, and could not form any true opinion as to whether or not the sisters resembled each other. The woman now leading a chanting band of feathered and painted five-year-olds in what appeared to be a war dance was in her late thirties, Katie guessed, with soft brown hair and deep-brown eyes. She wore no make-up, not even lipstick. She had on a plain blue smock and Reeboks with no socks. She was also wearing a huge feathered head-dress. Calling a break, she told Katie that this was an authentic Lakota Sioux ritual rain dance, and that she and the children were trying to break the twenty-seven day drought that had gripped the region.

'Keeps the foliage on the trees,' she said, 'but the reservoirs are down some fifty percent.' She waved her feathered dancers toward a long wooden table upon which pint cartons of milk and platters of cookies had been set out. Keeping a constant eye on the children, she walked Katie to a nearby bench, where they sat side by side in dappled shade.

'Did your sister ever mention her visits to a priest at Our Lady of Sorrows?' Katie asked.

'No,' Helen said at once, and turned toward her, surprised. 'Why would she go there? Her church is St Matthew's.'

'The priest indicated that something was troubling her. Would she have mentioned that to you?'

'No. But why is it important?'

Katie explained what a possible defense tactic might be. Helen listened intently, shaking her head, occasionally sighing. At last, she said, 'That's absurd, nothing was troubling my sister that deeply. Nothing she confided to me, anyway. Well ... but no.'

'What?'

'She and Andy were trying to have a baby. Without any luck.'

'Would that have bothered her enough to ...?'

'Well, Andy's *attitude* might have annoyed her. But I don't think she'd have gone to a priest about it.'

'What attitude?'

'He didn't want a "damn baby", as he put it. Went along with her efforts only because she threatened to leave him if he didn't. But they argued day and night about it, even when other people were with them. He kept saying if they had a damn baby, they'd never be able to go back to Europe the way he wanted to. He studied art in Europe, you know, and his big dream was to go back there. That's what he'd been saving for, and having a baby would ruin all that. I sometimes felt the reason she couldn't conceive was because of Andy's negative stance. I know that's dumb, but it's what I thought.'

'But she never once mentioned seeing Father McDowell?'

'No.'

'Never mentioned whatever was troubling her?'

'Never.' She was silent for a moment, and then suddenly, as if the idea had just occurred to her, she asked, 'Have you looked for a diary?'

'No, did she keep...?'

'Why don't you look for a diary or something?' Helen said. 'She always kept a diary when we were kids. Little lock on it, kept it in her top dresser drawer, under her socks. I'll bet anything she *still* keeps one, you really should take a look.' And then, all at once, she realized that she was speaking of her sister in the present tense, as if she were still alive. Her eyes clouded. 'Well, we were kids,' she said, and fell silent.

Across the yard, the children were beginning to get restless. 'This whole damn thing,' she said, shaking her head, 'the damn *stupidity* of it ... the ... the very *idea* that some smart lawyer might try to get Andy off on a ridiculous claim of ... of ... Mary Beth being *troubled*!'

She rose abruptly.

'Send him away,' she said. 'Send the son of a bitch away for life.' Katie was about to explain yet another time that all you could get for vehicular homicide was a maximum of seven years. But Helen had already turned away, and in an overly loud voice she shouted, 'OK, let's make *rain*!'

The request Katie typed into her computer read:

1. I am a detective of the River Close Police Department, assigned to the Raleigh Station, where I am currently investigating the vehicular homicide of Mary Beth Newell.
2. I have information based upon facts supplied to me by Father Brian McDowell, pastor of the Church of Our Lady of Sorrows in River Close, that Mrs Newell had been coming to him 'for spiritual guidance' regarding personal problems.
3. I have information based upon facts supplied to me by Mrs Helen Pierce, the deceased's sister, that she kept a locked personal diary in the top drawer of her...

Well, now, she thought, leave us pause a moment, shall we? Am I telling the absolute truth here? On an affidavit that will be sworn to before a magistrate? True, Helen Pierce told me her sister *used* to keep a locked diary when she was a kid, *used* to keep it in the top drawer of her dresser, is what Helen told me, Your Honor, I swear to that on a stack of bibles.

But she also said, and I quote this verbatim, 'I'll bet anything she *still* keeps one, you really should take a look,' is what she told me. Those were her exact words. So, whereas I *do* fervently wish to send Andrew Newell away for a very long time, the son of a bitch, I don't think I'm lying or even stretching the truth here when I say that I have information – based on facts supplied by her sister, Your Honor – that Mary Beth Newell kept a locked personal diary in the top drawer of her dresser, although not under her socks.

So, Your Honor...

Based upon the foregoing reliable information and upon my own personal knowledge, there is probable cause to believe that Mrs Newell may have confided to her diary information regarding her state of mind at the time of the incident, which information would help determine whether Mrs Newell was sufficiently troubled or distracted to have recklessly contributed in some measure to her own demise.

Which is exactly what Newell's lawyers would love to prove, and that's why I want to get my hands on that diary, if it exists, before they do, Your Honor.

Wherefore, I respectfully request that the court issue a search warrant in the form annexed hereto, authorizing a search of the premises at 1220 Hanover Road, Apartment 4C, for a diary belonging to the deceased.

They tossed the apartment high and low and could not find a locked diary in Mary Beth's top dresser drawer or anyplace else. They did, however, find an appointment calendar.

In plain view, as they would later tell Alyce Hart.

Which meant they were within their rights to seize the calendar as evidence without violating the court order.

The calendar revealed that starting on the twenty-first day of August, Mary Beth Newell had scheduled appointments at two fifteen every Wednesday and Saturday afternoon, with someone she'd listed only as 'McD'. These meetings continued through to the day of the accident.

'Well, even beyond that,' Katie said. 'Take a look. She had another one scheduled for tomorrow, and another two next week. Now unless she was going to McDonald's for hamburgers, I think we can safely assume the 'McD' stands for McDowell. In which case...'

'Let's revisit the man,' Carl said.

Father McDowell was alone in a small chapel off the side portal, deep in silent prayer when they entered the church through the center doors at three that afternoon. A blazing afternoon sun illuminated the high arched stained-glass windows, washing the aisles with color. They spotted the priest at once, and waited respectfully until he made the sign of the cross and got to his feet. He stood staring at the crucifix over the altar for a moment, as though not quite finished with his Lord and Savior, adding a postscript to his prayers, so to speak, and then made the sign of the cross again, and started backing away into the main church. He turned, saw them at once, scowled with the memory of their earlier visit, and seemed ready to make a dash for the safety of the church proper – but they were upon him too swiftly; he was trapped in the tiny chapel.

'Few questions, Father,' Katie said at once.

'I have business to attend to,' he said.

'So do we,' Carl said.

'We have Mary Beth Newell's appointment calendar,' Katie said. 'It shows she'd been coming to see you twice a week since the third week in August.'

Father McDowell said nothing.

'That sounds pretty serious to us,' Carl said. 'A woman walking all the way over here, twice a week.'

'What was troubling her, Father?'

'We need to know.'

58

'Why?' he asked.

'Did Andrew Newell know she was coming here?'

From the organ loft, quite abruptly, there came the sound of thick sonorous notes, flooding the church. The glorious music, the sunlight streaming through the stained glass, the scent of incense burning somewhere, the flickering of votive candles in small red containers on the altar behind McDowell, all blended to lend the small church the sudden air of a medieval cathedral, where knights in armor came to say their last confessions before riding off to battle.

'Why was she coming to see you?' Katie asked.

'Why not her own parish?' Carl asked.

'Help us, Father,' Katie said.

'Why?' he asked again.

'Because if her husband knew she was coming here, if he *knew* his wife was troubled about something...'

'Then his attorney might try to show she was distracted at the time of the accident...'

'... walked into that car because her mind was on something else.'

'Worse yet, walked into it *deliberately*.'

'She was not suicidal, if that's what you're suggesting,' McDowell said.

'Then tell us *what* she was.'

'Help us,' Katie said again.

The priest sighed heavily.

'Please,' she said.

He nodded, almost to himself, nodded again and then walked into the church proper, up the center aisle to a pew some six rows back from the main altar. The detectives sat one on either side of him. As he spoke, McDowell kept his eyes on the crucifix hanging above the altar, as if begging forgiveness for breaking faith with someone who had come to him in confidence. From the organ loft, the music swelled magnificently. McDowell spoke in a whisper that cut through the laden air like a whetted knife.

'She came to see me because she suspected her husband was having an affair,' he said. 'She was too embarrassed to go to her parish priest.'

But twice a week? Katie thought. For eight weeks? Ever since the twenty-first of August?

As McDowell tells it, at first she is uncertain, blaming herself for being a suspicious wife, wondering if her doubts have more to do with her inability to become pregnant than with what she perceives as her husband's wandering. He doesn't want a baby, she knows that; he has made that abundantly clear to her. As the weeks go by and she becomes more and more convinced that he is cheating on her, she wonders aloud and tearfully if perhaps her incessant campaign, her relentless attempts to conceive, her strict insistence on observing the demands of the calendar and the thermometer chart, haven't transmogrified what should have been a pleasurable act into an onerous experience, something dutiful and distasteful, something rigid and structured that has forced him to seek satisfaction elsewhere.

'By the end of the summer, she was positive there was another woman,' McDowell said.

'Did she say who?'

'No. But she was becoming very frightened.'

'Why?'

'Because someone was following her.'

'She saw someone following her?'

'No, she didn't actually *see* anyone. But she felt a presence behind her. Watching her every move.'

'A presence?' Carl asked, raising his eyebrows skeptically.

'Yes,' McDowell said. 'Someone behind her. Following her.'

'Good!' Alyce said on the telephone that evening. 'This only makes him more despicable!'

'You think he was the one following her?' Katie asked.

'Either him or his bimbo, who cares? Here's a woman trying to get pregnant and her darling husband's fooling around. Just *let* the defense try to show her as a troubled woman – I dare them. The trouble was her *husband*. Gets into a car stoned out of his mind and causes the death of an innocent wife who's faithfully attempting to create a family while he's running around with another woman. Seven years? The jury will want to *hang* him!'

Katie hoped she was right.

'Let's nail it down,' Alyce said. 'I want a minute by minute timetable, Katie. I want to know who saw the training car leaving the school parking lot at exactly what time. Who served Andrew Newell that Coke at exactly what time. Who saw Mary Beth Newell step out of that church and start walking toward her rendezvous with death at exactly what time...'

Sounding like she was already presenting her closing argument to the jury...

'... who saw the car approaching the crossing of Third and Grove at exactly what time. Who saw the car striking that poor woman at exactly what time. It takes fifteen to thirty minutes for Seconal to start working. OK, let's prove to a jury that he had to've swallowed the drug on the way to Grove and Third and was incapable of preventing his own wife's death! Lets prove the cheating bastard *killed* her!'

Amen, Katie thought.

The accident had taken place on Wednesday at approximately three twenty in the afternoon. This was now eleven a.m. on Saturday morning, the nineteenth day of October, and the drive-in at this hour was virtually deserted, the breakfast crowd having already departed, the lunch crowd not yet here.

Katie and Carl asked to see the manager and were told by a sixteen-year-old kid wearing a red and yellow uniform that the manager was conducting a training session just now and wouldn't be free for ten, fifteen minutes. Carl told her to inform the manager that the police were here. They ordered coffee and donuts at the counter, and carried them to one of the booths. The manager came out some three minutes later.

She was nineteen or twenty, Katie guessed, a pert little black woman with a black plastic name tag that told them she was JENNIE DEWES, MGR. She slid in the booth alongside Carl, looked across at Katie, and said, 'What's the trouble?'

'No trouble,' Katie said. 'We're trying to pinpoint the exact time a Coca Cola would have been purchased here on Wednesday afternoon.'

Jennie Dewes, Mgr looked at her.

'You're kidding, right?' she said.

'No, we're serious, miss,' Carl said.

'You know how many Cokes we serve here every day?'

'This would've been a Coke you served sometime around three o'clock this past Wednesday,' Katie said.

'You mind if I see your badges, please?' Jennie said.

Katie opened her handbag, fished out her shield in its leather fob. Carl had already flipped open his wallet.

'Okay,' Jennie said, and nodded. 'This would've been drive-in or counter?'

'Drive-in,' Katie said.

'Three o'clock would've been Henry on the window. Let me get him.'

She left the booth, and returned some five minutes later with a lanky young blond boy who looked frightened.

'Sit down, son,' Carl said.

The boy sat. Sixteen, seventeen years old, Katie guessed, narrow acne-ridden face, blue eyes wide in fear. Jennie sat, too. Four of them in the booth now. Jennie sitting beside Carl, Henry on Katie's left.

'We're talking about three days ago,' Carl said. 'Blue Ford Escort with a student driver plate on it, would you remember?'

'No, sir, I'm sorry, I sure don't,' Henry said.

'Don't be scared, Henry,' Katie said. 'You're not in any trouble here.'

'I'm not scared, ma'am,' he said.

'Blue Ford Escort. Yellow and black student driver plates on the front and rear bumper.'

'Young blonde girl would've been driving.'

'Pulled in around three, ordered a Coke.'

'Not at the window,' Jennie said suddenly.

They all looked at her.

'If this is the right girl, I saw her inside here. Pretty white girl, blonde, sixteen, seventeen years old.'

'Sixteen, yes. Brown eyes.'

'Didn't notice her eyes.'

'Man with her would've been older.'

'Thirty-two.'

'Wasn't any man with her when I saw her.'

'What time was this?' Katie asked.

'Around three, like you say. She was coming out of the ladies' room. Went to the counter to pick up her order.'

'Picked up a Coke at the counter?'

'*Two* of them was what she picked up. Two medium Cokes.'

They found her at a little past noon in the River Close Public Library, poring over a massive volume of full-color Picasso prints. The table at which she sat was huge and oaken, with green-shaded lamps casting pools of light all along its length. There was a hush to the room. Head bent, blonde hair cascading over the open book, Rebecca did not sense their approach until they were almost upon her. She reacted with a startled gasp, and then recovered immediately.

'Hey, hi,' she said.

'Hello, Rebecca,' Katie said.

Carl merely nodded.

The two detectives sat opposite her at the table. A circle of light bathed the riotous Picasso print, touched

Rebecca's pale hands on the open book, and Carl's darker hands flat on the table top.

'Rebecca,' Katie said, 'what happened to the second Coke container?

'What?' Rebecca said, and blinked.

'You bought two Cokes,' Carl said. 'The techs found only one empty container in the car. What happened to the other one?'

'I guess I threw it out,' Rebecca said.

'Then there *were* two containers, right?'

'I guess so. Yes, there probably were.'

'Why'd you throw it out?' Katie asked.

'Well ... because I'd finished with it.'

'Rebecca ... the container you threw out wasn't yours, was it?'

'Yes, it was. I'm sorry, I don't know what you're ...'

'It was Mr Newell's, wasn't it?'

'No, I distinctly remember...'

'The one *he* was drinking from, isn't that true?'

'No, that was in the holder. The cup holder. On the center console. I'm sorry, but I'm not following you. If you can tell me what you're looking for, maybe I can help you. But if you...'

'Where'd you toss the container?' Carl asked.

'Somewhere on the ... the street, I guess. I really don't remember.'

'Where on the street?'

'I don't remember the exact location. I just opened the window and threw it out.'

'Was it somewhere between the drive-in and the spot where you ran down Mrs Newell?'

'I suppose so.'

'We'll look for it,' Carl said.

'We'll find it,' Katie said.

'So find it,' Rebecca said. 'What's so important about a stupid *Coke* container, anyway?'

'The residue,' Katie said.

And suddenly Rebecca was weeping.

The way she tells it...

This was after she'd been informed of her rights, and after her attorney and her father had both warned her, begged her not to answer any questions.

But she tells it, anyway.

She is sixteen, and so she must tell it.

The video camera whirs silently as the little blonde girl with the wet brown eyes tells the camera and her lawyer and her father and the state attorney and all the assembled police officers exactly how this thing came to pass.

She supposes she fell in love with Mr Newell...

She keeps referring to him as 'Mr Newell'. She does not call him Andrew or Andy, which is odd when one considers the intimate nature of their relationship. But he remains 'Mr Newell' throughout her recitation.

Mr Newell and his passionate love of art, which he transmits to his students in a very personal way, 'What do you see? What do you see *now*?'

And, oh, what she sees is this charming, educated man, much older than she is, true, but seeming so very *young*, burning with enthusiasm and knowledge, this sophisticated world traveler who studied in Italy and in France and who is now trapped in a shoddy little town like River Close with a wife who can only think of making babies!

She doesn't learn this, doesn't hear about his wife's ... well, obsession, you might call it ... until she begins taking driving lessons with him at the beginning of August. They are alone together for almost two hours each time, twice a week, and she feels confident enough to tell him all about her dreams and her desires, feels privileged when he confides to her his plans of returning to Europe one day, to Italy especially, where the light is golden and soft.

'Like you, Rebecca,' he says to her one day, and puts his hand on her knee and dares to kiss her, dares to slide his hand up under her short skirt.

There are places in River Close...

There are rivers and lakes and hidden glades where streams are drying in the hot summer sun, no rain, the trees thick with leaves. The little blue Ford Escort hidden from prying eyes while Mr Newell gives her lessons of quite another sort. Rebecca open and spread beneath him on the back seat. Mr Newell whispering words of encouragement and endearment while he takes her repeatedly, twice a week. Rebecca delirious with excitement and wildly in love.

When she suggests one day toward the middle of September...

They are in a parched hidden glade; if only it would rain, the town needs rain so badly. Her panties are off, she is on the back seat; they have already made love, and she feels flushed and confident. He is telling her he adores her, worships her, kissing her again, calling her his blonde princess, his little blonde princess. I love you, I love you, kissing her everywhere, everywhere...

'Then leave your wife and marry me,' she suggests. 'Take me with you to Italy.'

'No, no,' he says, 'I can't do that.'

'Why not?' she says. 'You love me, don't you?'

'I adore you,' he says.

'Then marry me.'

'I can't,' he says.

'Why not?' she asks again.

'I'm already married,' he says.

There is a smile on his face as he makes his little joke – I'm already married – which is supposed to explain it all to the little sophomore who was stupid enough to fall in love with the worldly art professor. How could she have been so goddamn *dumb*?

What do you see, Rebecca?

What do you see *now*?

She sees killing her.

Mr Andrew Newell's beloved wife Mary Beth.

'At first, I could only follow her on Saturdays. I go to school, you know. But I had to figure out a way to kill her with the *car*, so he'd be blamed. I take Driver's Ed courses so I knew that the licensed driver is the one responsible in any accident. So I wanted him to be in the car with me, so he'd be blamed. That way he'd be charged with murder and get sent to prison for life.

'But I needed to know where she'd be on the days I had my driving lessons, Wednesdays and Fridays. So one week, I stayed home from school and followed her on Wednesday. She went to the church again, same as on Saturday. And the next week I stayed home on Friday and followed her, but she was just doing errands and such, it would've been too difficult to plan a way our paths would intersect. Her path and the car's path, I mean. During a driving lesson. A Wednesday driving lesson. It had to be on a Wednesday, because that's when she went to the church, you see.

'I take Driver's Ed courses, I know all about drunk driving, I figured the only way Mr Newell could be blamed was if I got him drunk. But he didn't drink. I once brought a bottle of wine to the woods with us, this was the second time we made love. I wanted to show him how sophisticated I was, so I bought this bottle of very expensive Chardonnay, it cost me twenty-two dollars. But he wouldn't drink any, he told me he didn't drink. That was when I still thought he loved me. That was before I realized he was making a fool of me.

'There are lots of medical books in my father's library – he's a doctor, you know – books on pharmacology and toxicology, everything I needed. I started browsing the books, trying to find something I could give Mr Newell that would make it *look* as if he was drunk when I ran her over. Make it look like *he* was the responsible party. Any of the barbiturates looked good to me. I searched through my father's bag one night and found some Seconal capsules and decided to go with them. I dropped two big red caps in his Coke before I carried it out to the car. Two hundred milligrams. I figured that would do it. The rest was easy.'

'Did you intend killing her?' Alyce asked.
  'Oh yes.'
  'Why?'
  'Because he was making a fool of me. He loved her, you see, otherwise he'd have left her to marry me. I did it to pay him back. If this worked the way I wanted it to, he'd have gone to prison for life.'

'Do you know what the penalty for vehicular homicide is?' Katie asked.

'Yes,' she said at once. 'Prison for life. Homicide is murder.'

'Seven years, Rebecca.'

Rebecca looked at her.

'It's seven years.'

The room went utterly still.

'I didn't know that,' Rebecca said.

'Well, now you do,' Alyce said.

It began raining along about then.

Driving home through the rain, Katie thought how goddamn sad it was that a girl as bright and as beautiful as Rebecca could have made the tragic mistake of believing in love and romance in a time when vows no longer meant anything.

Sixteen years old, she thought. Only sixteen.

I'm in love with someone else, Katie.

I'm leaving you.

The irony, she thought, and brushed hot sudden tears from her eyes.

'Enough,' she said aloud.

And drove fiercely into the storm ahead.